Dear mouse friends,
Welcome to the world of

Geronimo Stilton

THE RODENT'S GAZETTE
EDITORIAL STAFF

Geronimo Stilton
A learned and brainy
mouse; editor of
The Rodent's Gazette

Thea Stilton
Geronimo's sister and
special correspondent at
The Rodent's Gazette

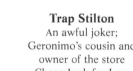

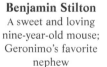

Trap Stilton
An awful joker;
Geronimo's cousin and
owner of the store
Cheap Junk for Less

Benjamin Stilton
A sweet and loving
nine-year-old mouse;
Geronimo's favorite
nephew

Geronimo Stilton

THE PHANTOM BANDIT

Scholastic Inc.

Copyright © 2016 by Edizioni Piemme S.p.A., Palazzo Mondadori, Via Mondadori 1, 20090 Segrate, Italy. International Rights © Atlantyca S.p.A. English translation © 2018 by Atlantyca S.p.A.

The publisher does not have any control over and does not assume any responsibility for author or third-party websites or their content.

GERONIMO STILTON names, characters, and related indicia are copyright, trademark, and exclusive license of Atlantyca S.p.A. All rights reserved. The moral right of the author has been asserted. Based on an original idea by Elisabetta Dami. geronimostilton.com

Published by Scholastic Inc., *Publishers since 1920,* 557 Broadway, New York, NY 10012. SCHOLASTIC and associated logos are trademarks and/or registered trademarks of Scholastic Inc.

Stilton is the name of a famous English cheese. It is a registered trademark of the Stilton Cheese Makers' Association. For more information, go to stiltoncheese.com.

No part of this publication may be reproduced, stored in a retrieval system, or transmitted in any form or by any means, electronic, mechanical, photocopying, recording, or otherwise, without written permission of the copyright holder. For information regarding permission, please contact: Atlantyca S.p.A., Via Leopardi 8, 20123 Milan, Italy; e-mail foreignrights@atlantyca.it, atlantyca.com.

ISBN 978-1-338-26853-9

Text by Geronimo Stilton
Original title *La notte delle Zucche Mannare*
Cover by Andrea Da Rold and Andrea Cavallini
Illustrations by Ivan Bigarella, Daria Cerchi, and Roberta Bianchi
Graphics by Michela Battaglin

Special thanks to Tracey West
Translated by Julia Heim
Interior design by Maria Mercado

10 9 8 7 6 5 4 3 2   18 19 20 21 22

Printed in the U.S.A.   40
First printing 2018

OH, HOW I LOVE FALL!

It was a beautiful **FALL** morning. It had just stopped **raining**, and my whiskers twitched at the smell of **damp** leaves mixed with the scent of **freshly baked** cheese pastries wafting from the café. I breathed in the cool, fresh air as I **pedaled** toward my office.

Wait, I almost forgot! My name is Stilton, *Geronimo Stilton*. I am the editor of *The Rodent's Gazette*, the most famous **newspaper** on Mouse Island.

What a beautiful day!

As I was saying, my dear rodent friends, I was really enjoying the BEAUTIFUL autumn air. I couldn't wait for the weekend. I planned to invite all my **friends** to the Stilton **farm**, out in the country. There, we could pick **CHESTNUTS** and **roast** them around a fire.

OH, HOW I LOVE FALL!

The leaves are so colorful, and it's the best season to eat grilled cheese!

When I reached 17 Swiss Cheese Center, I parked my bicycle in front. On the way to my office, I passed by the break room. There, **MUNCHING** on cheese, I saw Vanessa Vogue (the *Gazette*'s fashion journalist); my sister, Thea; (the *Gazette*'s special correspondent); and Cara DeColores (the graphic designer for the *Gazette*).

They were all whispering mysteriously, "PSSST . . . DID YOU HEAR?"

"PSSST . . . everyone will be there . . . PSSSST . . . it will be scary, scream-worthy, a real frightfest!"

Hmmm . . . strange!

Psst . . . . psssssssst . . .

Psssst . . . I heard . . .

PSSSST . . . PSSST . . . PSSST . . .

I interrupted them. "Hello, everyone!" I said. "What exactly are you saying is going to be **SCARY**, **SCREAM-WORTHY**, and **frightening**?"

The three rodents looked **startled** to see me.

"Why, um, we were just talking about a new article idea I just had," Vanessa answered. "About the, um, **frightening** new fashions in Transylmousea."

"That sounds **mousetastic**!" I said. "**Good luck** with the article!"

They all quickly stood up.

"Thanks, Geronimo!" Thea said. "But, um, it's late and we need to get back to work!"

Then they **ran off**, and I was confused. Why were they in such a rush?

WHAT A STRANGE ENCOUNTER!

T . . . PSSST . . . PSSST... PSSST...

Pssst . . .

Pssst . . .

Huh?!

On the second floor, I spotted my **assistant**, Mousella, chatting with reporter Babs Bonbon.

"**PSSST**," she said in a loud whisper. "Everyone will be there . . . **PSSST** . . . it will be scary, scream-worthy, a real frightfest!"

I interrupted them, too. "Excuse me, but what is going to be **SCARY, SCREAM-WORTHY**, and **frightening**?"

"Um, we were just talking about the new horror film, The Ghost of Cheddar Castle," Mousella explained. "Sorry, we have to get back to work!" Then they both scurried away.

ANOTHER STRANGE ENCOUNTER!

I ran into Jim Dribbles (the *Gazette*'s

expert **Soccer** commentator) who was whispering with his sister Gloria.

"**PSSST**," Jim whispered. "Everyone will be there. **PSSST**. . . it will be scary, scream-worthy, and a real frightfest!"

"Excuse me, friends," I asked. "Can you **PLEASE** tell me what is going to be scary, scream-worthy, and frightening?"

Jim's eyes got wide, and he pointed. "That piece of flying cheese right behind you!"

"What? Flying cheese?" I asked.

Ha, ha, ha!

Flying cheese!

Huh?

Confused, I turned my head, but there was nothing behind me! When I turned back, Jim and Gloria were **running** away, giggling.

"**GERONIMO HAS BEEN SUCCESSFULLY DISTRACTED!**" Jim was saying to his sister. "The secret has been protected! And it was will be truly **SCARY, SCREAM-WORTHY**, and **frightening**!"

How strange! I tried to follow them, but they were in much better shape than I was and I couldn't catch up.

THAT WAS MY THIRD STRANGE ENCOUNTER IN A ROW!

Jim had used the word *secret*. Now it was clear that my coworkers were **hiding** something from me. But what could it be?

I needed some fresh air to clear my head. But when I opened my office window, what I saw made my whiskers shake!

A long black car marked **Funeral Movers** was parked in front of the building.

Some rodents dressed in black were unloading **coffin-shaped** boxes.

THIS WAS THE STRANGEST ENCOUNTER OF THEM ALL!

I **quickly** ran downstairs to see what they were up to. As I passed by the cafeteria, my nose twitched. The smell of cheesy goodness wafted through the doors. But who was cooking so early?

HOW STRANGE!

I started to push open the doors, but a **furry** paw pushed me back.

"Geronimo, why are you being so **nosy**?"

Who's cooking?

"**Eeeeeek!**" I squeaked.

Then I realized that it was just my cousin Trap.

"**Don't call me nosy!**" I snapped. "Strange things are happening around here, and I am the ⓄⓃⓁⓎ ⓄⓃⒺ who doesn't know what's going on!"

I tried to look past him, but he kept moving his body, **BLOCKING** my view. Then he started to tease me by singing a silly song.

"Geroni-mini is a curious **ninny**! Geroni-mad is a curious **LAD**! Geroni-mule is a curious **FOOL**!"

A STRESS-FREE VACATION!

I left Trap and ran outside to try to find out what the **gloomy** movers were doing. But there was no sign of them, or the **coffin-shaped** boxes.

VERY STRANGE!

All of the **mysterious** happenings at *The Rodent's Gazette* were making me uneasy. I headed back home and saw that my **DOOR** was slightly open!

oh no! Was there a thief inside?

With trembling paws, I opened the door.

Who's in there?

Inside my living room sat my sister, Thea; **Mousita Middleton**, who works at the newspaper; and my friend **CREEPELLA VON CRACKLEFUR**. They were whispering to one another.

"**PSST** . . . let's get rid of him for a while," Thea was saying.

WHAT A STRANGE SCENE!

"Holey cheese!" I cried. "How did you all get in here? I almost **FAINTED** with fright!"

"Calm down," Thea said. "I used the spare key you gave me."

"We just came to check on you, Gerrykins," Creepella said. "Trap told us you were acting **STRANGE**."

"I'm not the one acting **STRANGE**!" I protested. "It's everyone else! Why is everyone

I'm not acting strange!

being **mysterious**? Everyone is whispering! And talking about scary things! And who were those **Funeral Movers** I saw?"

Exhausted, I plopped down on my chair.

Creepella patted my head. "Poor Gerrykins. You're very **stressed**!"

Mousita jumped up. "I'll make you some **SOOTHING** tea!"

Creepella whispered in my ear. "You need a little stress-free vacation, Gerrykins."

"Hmm," I said. "A stress-free vacation sounds nice."

She clapped her paws together. "**Perfect!**" she cried. "You can come with me to **CACKLEFUR CASTLE**!"

Cacklefur Castle? There was nothing relaxing about that spooky place!

"Well, actually, I can't . . ." I started to protest, but Creepella was already shouting into her phone.

"Geronimo Stilton will be coming with me to the **castle** for a short vacation," she said. "Prepare the **best** room for him, Boneham! Yes, Geronimo, that sweet little **SCAREDY-RAT** who has a big *crush* on me."

"Well, actually, I don't have a cr —" I

tried to explain, but Creepella had already grabbed MY PAW and was leading me outside.

Mousita gave me a **thermos** of tea, and Thea shoved a pre-packed suitcase into my paw.

As I climbed into the car, I could swear I heard Thea whisper, "It will be SCARY, scream-worthy, and a real frightfest!"

NOT AGAIN! HOW STRANGE!

But before I could ask her any questions, Creepella's Turbotomb *sped* away.

I Am Not
a Jealous Mouse!

We arrived at **cacklefur castle** at the stroke of midnight —

the witching hour!

I had seen the castle many times before, but it still gave me **chills** whenever I saw it. It stood upon a **skull-shaped** hill, and its **TALL** spires extended into the **dark** sky.

To make things even creepier, a terrible **STORM** had broken out just as we got there. **Lightning** bolts flashed, **thunder** boomed, and an eerie wind whistled through the spooky trees.

THE HEADLESS
GHOST ROOM

THE TOWER OF THE
HEADLESS GHOST

DINING ROOM

THE KITCHEN

THE WEREWOLF
PUMPKIN GARDEN

CREEPELLA'S ROOM

THE VON CACKLEFUR FAMILY

CHEF STEWRAT

SHIVEREEN

KAFKA

CREEPELLA VON CACKLEFUR

MADAME LATOMB

BABY

GRANDPA FRANKENSTEIN

BONEHAM

SNIP AND SNAP

BITEWING

BORIS
VON CACKLEFUR

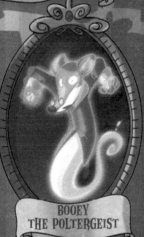

BOOEY
THE POLTERGEIST

GRANDMA
CRYPT

CHOMPERS

When I got out of the car I was greeted by the castle's butler, **Boneham**.

"Welcome, Mr. Geronimo," he said. Then he lowered his voice to a whisper. "Of all the **guests** tonight, you are the nicest."

Welcome!

Thanks!

I was **surprised**. I didn't know there would be other **rodents** on my stress-free vacation.

"Um, what **guests**?" I asked.

Then I noticed a rodent bending over the moat, collecting drops of **SLIME** in a test tube. It was the famouse professor **Alvin Testerly**, who had just won the **Rodel Prize in Science**!

He walked over to Creepella and **kissed** her paw. "You are truly **enchanting**, my

dear host," he said. "Thank you for letting me study the SLIME in your moat. It will come in handy to my research on ghostly superviruses."

Creepella smiled. "I am **happy** to do my part to advance science!" she replied.

Then I heard Boneham whisper in my ear, "Please don't be jealous, Mr. Geronimo. Lady Creepella only has **EYES** for you!" "**JEALOUS? WHO, ME?**" I asked. "**NO, I'M JUST A LITTLE BIT HUNGRY.**"

Creepella overheard me. "Hungry? Then why don't you and I have a midnight snack of Chef Stewrat's **stew**, Gerrykins?"

The thought of that terrible stew made my whiskers twitch. Before I could refuse, a luxury sports car pulled up next to the Turbotomb.

A tall rodent in an elegant suit and **purple** bow tie stepped out of the car. It was the famous **FILM DIRECTOR**, Gaspar Ghostine!

I knew that Gaspar had won a Mouscar award for **Best Spooky Film** for his movie **The Muenster Under the Bed**. He had brought Creepella a big bouquet of purple roses. "For you, my dear," he said. "Thank you for allowing me to film my next movie, The Gorgonzola Ghost, at your castle."

"How **thoughtful**!" Creepella exclaimed. "Boneham, please put these in a nice vase."

Humph!   How thoughtful!   For you!

"All those roses! What a show-off!" I snorted.

"Please don't be *jealous*, Mr. Geronimo," Boneham repeated. "Lady Creepella only has **EYES** for you."

"**JEALOUS? WHO, ME?**" I replied. "**NO, I'M JUST A LITTLE BIT COLD.**"

Creepella took my paw. "Let's go inside, Gerrykins. We can sit by the fire and warm up."

We entered the castle, where we ran into a rodent with green fur...

Meet the new gardener!

IT WAS GRANDPA FRANKENSTEIN!

Creepella's grandfather was chatting with a **muscular** rodent wearing a gardener's apron and ROUND sunglasses. His green shirt had a pattern of colorful Flowers, and his pants were stained with dirt.

"Meet the new GARDENER, Felix Bloomfur," Grandpa said. "He will manage our greenhouse of carnivorous plants."

Felix turned to greet us and STARED at Creepella, his face as red as a tomato. "C-C-Creepella von Cacklefur? Is th-th-that really you?" he asked. "You look even more enchanting than you do in pictures. I c-c-can't believe I'm actually MEETING you!"

It's you!

"Can I have your phone number? What are you doing tonight? Are you dating anyone?"

She pulled a purple notebook out of her bag. "Why don't you give me your phone number, and I'll add it to the guest book," she said politely. "That way I can call you one day (or maybe not)."

"HUMPH!" I snorted. How rude of Felix to ask for her phone number like that!

Grandpa Frankenstein winked at me. "Don't be jealous, Geronimo," he said.

"JEALOUS? WHO, ME?" I replied. "NO, I AM JUST A LITTLE BIT TIRED FROM THE TRIP."

"Why don't you rest a little before we eat, Gerrykins?" Creepella asked.

Then Boneham appeared. "Please, guests, FOLLOW me," the butler said. "I will take you to your room."

We had started to walk up a dark **staircase** when I saw Creepella drop her purple notebook. I glanced at it and saw that it had a **golden** lock and some words written on the front. It wasn't a **guest book** at all!

Follow me!

My diary!

It was her secret diary!

She saw me looking at it **curiously**, and she smiled.

"I keep track of my **ADMIRERS** in here, and all the gifts they give me so I can send them thank-you notes," she said. "You can **LOOK** at it, but don't be jealous."

"**I AM NOT A JEALOUS MOUSE!**" I insisted.

Jealous? Who, me?

Don't be jealous!

Secret Diary of
CREEPELLA
VON CACKLEFUR

Paws off, or I will
mummify you!

MY ADMIRERS

HAT

GLOVES

Sal Cemeterius

Glen Ghoulson

SWEETS

RING

Baron von Slick

SERVANT

Prince Harold the Horrible

Count Sylvania

FLOWERS

Gaspar Ghostine

Alvin Testerly

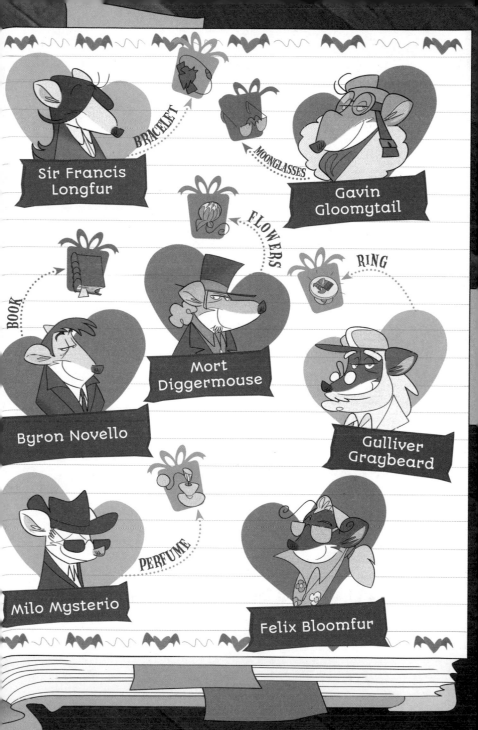

THE ROOM OF THE
HEADLESS GHOST

Boneham stopped at the top of the stairs.

"Mr. Geronimo, this is your room," he said. "The Room of the Headless Ghost. It is the scariest, most frightening room in the entire castle! I hope you are pleased."

"Th-th-thanks," I stammered. But I wasn't pleased. I was terrified.

The door opened with a creak. **Creeeaaak!**

I let out a scared squeak. **Squeeeaaak!**

Then I stepped inside. **Eeeeeeeek!**

Purple satin covered the walls, which made the room look very gloomy. In the center was a long canopy bed with purple sheets, and **bats** carved into the tops of the posts.

Flames danced in the marble fireplace, projecting long, eerie **SHADOWS** on the walls. They lit up a brass plaque on an old suit of armor.

> ARMOR OF THE DECEASED
> COUNT BRAGSBY VON CACKLEFUR, KNOWN AS
> ## THE HEADLESS GHOST

Suddenly, the suit of armor moved! I jumped back. The arm lifted and took off the helmet. I let out a **terrified** shriek. "Eeeeeeeeeek!"

"Do not be afraid, Geronimo!" a ghostly voice said. "I, the Headless Ghost, will watch over you as you sleep."

"Um, th-th-thanks," I stammered. "Although I do not think I will get any sleep in this room!"

EEEEEEEEEK!

I had been in many spooky rooms in the castle before, and I SHOULD HAVE BEEN USED TO THIS.

I decided to walk around before our late-night dinner. I knew I would run into more ghosts, monsters, and creatures, but I had to get away from that HEADLESS HORROR!

My whiskers twitched nervously as I

walked quickly through the castle's **DARK** hallways. I had a creepy feeling that I was being watched.

BOOEY

The **portraits** of the Cacklefur ancestors were following me with their eyes. What a fright! I had seen them before, so **I SHOULD HAVE BEEN USED TO THEM**.

Then another *ghost* appeared out of thin air. It was **Booey** the Poltergeist!

I knew Booey, and I should have been used to him, but I still **squeaked** in fright!

I heard a loud noise, and I nearly jumped out of my fur. Then I realized it was just Boneham banging the gong for dinner. I should have been used to that, but my nerves were on edge!

I kept walking, and something skittered across my foot. **Eeek!**

But it was just Kafka, the Cacklefurs' pet cockroach. I should have been used to him!

I kept walking through the halls, and then I heard an eerie voice behind me.

"Geronimooooo! Steer cleeeeeear of the werewolf pumpkins or I will gobble you up in one bite. MeOWWWW!"

I turned very slowly, and saw the SHADOW of a giant feline! I WAS DEFINITELY NOT USED TO THAT!

HEEEEEEEELP!

I screamed at the top of my rodent lungs!

"Heeeeelp!" I wailed as I *ran* all the way to the dining room. Most of the other guests were already seated.

"Gerrykins, what's wrong?" Creepella asked.

"Don't tell me you're still afraid of this castle," said Boris von Cacklefur, Creepella's dad. "YOU SHOULD BE USED TO IT BY NOW!"

"I have never seen a cat phantom before," I replied. "How could I be used to it?"

Creepella gasped. "A cat phantom? Are you sure?"

"Of course I'm sure!" I yelled. "It was terrifying! **Horrifying!** Eeeeeek!"

And then I fainted!

THE LEGEND OF THE WEREWOLF PUMPKINS

A **stinky stench** hit my nostrils and woke me up. I opened my eyes to see **CHEF STEWRAT** carrying a heavy **CAULDRON** and singing . . .

Time for stew!

I'VE GOT THE STEW!
IT'S TIME TO EAT!
I'VE MADE FOR YOU
A TASTY TREAT!

I'VE ADDED BUGS
LIKE FLIES AND WORMS
AND SPIDERS, SLUGS,
AND LOTS OF GERMS!

A MUMMY'S TOOTH,
A DAB OF DROOL,
HERE IS THE TRUTH:
MY STEW WILL RULE!

I almost **fainted** again, but Creepella fanned me with a napkin until I stopped feeling so dizzy.

"Gerrykins, do the ingredients of the stew still turn your stomach? **YOU SHOULD BE USED TO IT!**" she said.

"It looks **TERRIFYING**," said Gaspar Ghostine with a pleased grin. "I should make a movie about it. **Night of the Living Stew**!"

At that moment, Felix Bloomfur came running in. "Sorry I'm late. I took a little nap." He sniffed the air. "What is that **DELICIOUS** smell?"

"It is the Cacklefur family stew," Chef Stewrat replied proudly. "It has been boiling in the same **CAULDRON** for thirty-three generations! Geronimo, have the first helping!"

What a dreary delight!

THE ANCIENT RECIPE FOR CHEF STEWRAT'S STEW

Gather the most disgusting ingredients you can find. Mix them together in a large cauldron until you have a batch of slimy, sickening mush. Let it sit out in the sun until flies start flying off (which means it smells just right). Cook it over a slow fire for thirty-three generations, stirring every three months, three days, and three hours. Add more disgusting ingredients as needed. If it gets too thick, add some broth made from a moldy sock. Flavor it with a few drops of cemetery dew and sprinkle with graveyard dust before serving. Goes great with moldy toast spread with snail slime!

The thought of eating that horrible stew made me sob. "Enough!" I cried. "I don't want to eat the stew! I don't want to **sleep** in a room with a headless ghost! And I don't want to be gobbled up by a cat phantom! This was supposed to be a stress-free vacation, but it's not!"

Creepella's father frowned. "Geronimo, we have never seen a cat phantom around here. Are you really sure that's what you saw?"

"I am **absolutely**, pawsitively sure," I replied. "It was an **ENORMOUSE** shadow with cat ears. It even meowed! And then it told me to stay away from the werewolf pumpkins."

The members of the **CACKLEFUR** family looked at one another.

"Gerrykins, you won't believe this, but

there happens to be an ancient family legend about **werewolf pumpkins** and cat pirates," Creepella said.

"Wh-wh-what?" I stammered. "What do cat pirates have to do with this?"

"I'll be Right Back," Creepella promised, and she returned a moment later holding an antique scroll.

Here's the legend!

"The **LEGEND** of the cat pirates is very old," she explained. "It dates back to the Middle Ages.

"LISTEN TO THIS . . ."

The Legend of the Werewolf Pumpkins

During the first great invasion of cat pirates, hordes of dangerous felines invaded all of Mouse Island.

When the cat pirates tried to invade Cacklefur Castle, they could not get past the pumpkin patch—because it was not an ordinary pumpkin patch. The pumpkins were werewolf pumpkins, and when the cat pirates attacked, they fought back.

They wrapped their tendrils around the cats, trapping them. They gnashed at the cats with their sharp teeth. Frightened, the cat pirates fled, and the castle was spared, but many werewolf pumpkins were smashed on that sad night.

The Cacklefurs have never forgotten the heroic acts of the werewolf pumpkins. They planted more pumpkins and kept the garden lovingly tended. And every year, they celebrate the werewolf pumpkins on Halloween Night.

Alvin Testerly stroked his **whiskers**. "Very interesting," he said. "I would like to examine the **dirt** in the garden to see if there are any **mutant viruses** that make the pumpkins so big, and so full of **BITE**."

"Fabumouse!" explained Gaspar Ghostine. "Maybe it will **INSPIRE** my next film!"

Boris nodded. "Excellent. Let us visit the garden after dinner."

"Just don't forget about my **DELICIOUS** dessert," added Chef Stewrat.

Stew Cream Puffs!

Flaky pastry balls stuffed with stew, coated with stew sauce, and topped with a cherry!

It must be a mutant virus . . .
I'll make a film!
Delicious!
It smells yummy!
No stew for me!
Here's dessert!
Ha, ha, ha!
Hee, hee, hee!

THE WEREWOLF PUMPKIN GARDEN!

It was almost dawn when we walked to the **Werewolf Pumpkin Garden**. To get there, we had to pass through the Cacklefur family **cemetery**.

As we walked among the **gloomy** tombstones, my whiskers *trembled* in fright.

Boris laughed. "The pumpkins rather like the tombstones. They keep one another company. Ha, ha, ha!"

"What's the **SCIENTIFIC** classification of the pumpkins?" asked Felix Bloomfur.

"They are an interesting and **rare** species," Boris replied. "*Pumpkinus voracious chomperitus.*"

Welcome to the Werewolf Pumpkin Garden

The *pumpkinus voracious chomperitus* has many unusual traits. Each pumpkin can grow to an enormouse size, towering over the average rodent. Their tendrils are so strong that when they wrap around something, they do not let go. And when they catch you, they can chomp on you with one of their thirty-three razor-sharp teeth. What makes them especially dangerous is that they can pull themselves up by their roots and chase after anyone or anything that tries to harm them. All of these traits make them perfect for guarding Cacklefur Castle!

"I believe I have heard of the *pumpkinus voracious chomperitus,*" Felix said. "Is it true that they have teeth?"

Boris grinned. "Yes," he replied. "**Lots** of them!"

We walked up to a tall iron **gate** that opened into a garden filled with **HUGE** pumpkins. They were all bigger than we were. It was an **impressive** sight!

"It's a shame such big pumpkins only grow here," Felix remarked. "Have you ever thought about **selling** them?"

"Of course not!" Creepella replied. "These pumpkins are special. They saved the Cacklefur family. We will never sell them!"

"Besides, they are too **dangerous,**" Boris added. "Ordinary gardeners would not know how to control them."

Creepella opened the gate.

"**Stay back!**" she warned us. "The pumpkins will **BITE** anyone who isn't a Cacklefur."

She approached one of the pumpkins and **hugged** it. "It's all right, my treasure. Nobody here will harm you."

She turned to us. "The pumpkins are very **intelligent**. They can **understand** what we say. And they can **communicate** using a special **alphabet**."

Don't worry!

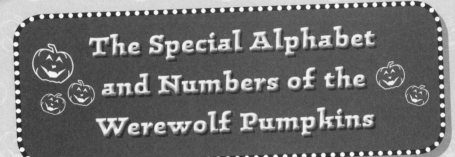

The Special Alphabet and Numbers of the Werewolf Pumpkins

A | B | C | D

E | F | G | H

I | J | K | L

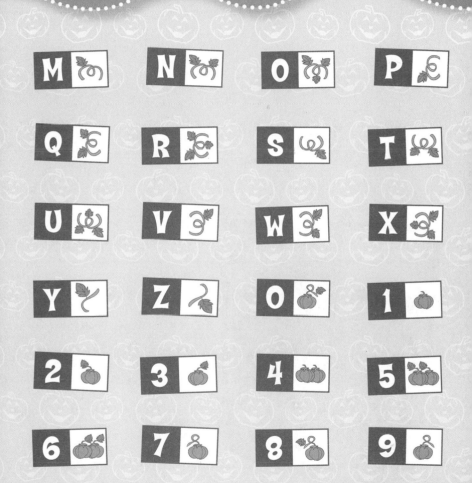

I'M A MOUSE,
NOT A PUMPKIN!

The **sun** had already risen when we returned to the castle.

"I'm dead tired," Creepella announced.

So tired!

"Everyone to bed, and gloomy dreams to all!"

I returned to my room and was so **tired** that I didn't care how spooky it was. I pulled the covers over me and tried to sleep.

But I couldn't sleep! First of all,

the **Headless Ghost** was snoring. *How could he* **snore** *without a head?* I wondered. But he was very loud. **Z-Z-Z-Z-Z-Z-Z-Z.**

Then some **crows** landed outside my window and began to caw. **CAAAW! CAAAW! CAAAW!**

Finally, my eyes drooped. I fell into a **DEEP SLEEP** and began to snore even louder than the Headless Ghost.

Z-Z-Z Z-Z-Z Z-Z-Z-Z-Z-Z-Z-Z-Z-Z!

I wasn't asleep for long when another sound woke me up. **CREEEEEAK!**

Someone had opened my door! **"WH-WH-WHO'S THERE?"** I stammered, but no one answered.

Then I heard footsteps walking toward my bed. **Tap, tap, tap!**

"Pssssst! Mr. Geronimoooooooo!"

I curled up into a terrified ball. **Squeeeak!**

Then I heard a **GHOSTLY** voice whisper, "Pssst! Mr. Geronimooo!"

Frozen in fright, I watched as a tall **shadow** moved across the curtains of the bed.

"**HEEEEELP!**" I yelled. "It's the Cat Phantom!"

"Nonsense, Mr. Geronimo," the shadow said. "It is I, Boneham. The sun is setting. Time to wake up!"

I groaned. This stunk worse than the

stinkiest cheese! "But I only just fell asleep!" I moaned. "I want to go back to bed!"

"That is not possible," Boneham said. "**MISS CREEPELLA** is waiting for you, and it is not a good idea to make her **wait** too long. Now eat your breakfast."

Boneham set a tray of **DISGUSTING** breakfast food before me. Stew tea, fresh-squeezed stew juice, a yogurt-and-stew smoothie, and a croissant filled with stew.

Breakfast!

I'm so tired!

I skipped breakfast and I went to see Creepella, yawning.

"**Wake up**, Gerrykins!" Creepella said cheerfully. "I have a hunch about the **Cat Phantom**. I think he might want to **steal** the werewolf pumpkins. Are you listening?"

But I had dozed off, hugging a statue. **Z-Z-Z-Z-Z-Z-Z!**

"**Waaaaaake uuuup!**" Creepella yelled.

My eyes flew open. "I'm awake. Full of pep and energy! Yawn . . ."

She handed me an **orange** costume. "Put this on," she insisted.

It was a **werewolf pumpkin** costume!

"I can't go around looking like this!" I protested. "**I'M A MOUSE, NOT A PUMPKIN!**"

"There are three reasons you need to wear this," Creepella said.

 1. The werewolf pumpkins will think you are one of them and won't bite you.

 2. The Cat Phantom will think you are a pumpkin, not a mouse.

 3. You will look totally adorable!

"You want me to wait for the **Cat Phantom** to show up?" I asked as I put on the costume, terrified.

"Yes," Creepella replied. "I even got you a pumpkin tent so you will be comfortable on your stakeout. **Good luck**, Gerrykins!"

A pumpkin tent!

Nom, Nom, Nom!

My whiskers **trembled** in fright as I tiptoed into the garden. The werewolf pumpkins didn't try to bite me.

GREAT GORGONZOLA, WAS I HAPPY TO BE WEARING THAT SILLY COSTUME!

There, done!

I quickly set up the pumpkin tent. It looked just like one of the enormouse werewolf pumpkins! The green cords that attached the tent to stakes in the ground looked like curly tendrils.

I settled in to wait. The sun had set, and the MOON shone overhead. I WAS SO SLEEPY! I yawned and entered the tent.

"I'll just take a little NAP," I said. "A teeny, tiny little NAP."

I quickly fell into a deep sleep.

Z-Z-Z Z-Z-Z-Z-Z Z-Z-Z-Z-Z-Z-Z-Z-Z!

I **snored** and **snored** late into the night. Then a noise startled me.

BOOOIIIIIING!
BOOOIIIIIING!

Someone (or something?) had tripped over the cords of the pumpkin tent! I **jumped** out of the tent.

"Who's there?" I squeaked.

Shaking like a tub of cottage cheese, and with my **fur** standing on end, I peeked out of the tent. The **full moon** lit up the night sky, as round and **pale** as a ball of mozzarella.

Then I saw it. The shadow of a **large cat**, swiftly moving through the garden.

"The ca . . . the ca-ca . . . the ca-ca-ca . . . the Cat Phantoooooom!" I stammered.

The Cat Phantom had tripped on the strings of the pumpkin tent! And now he had HEARD me and was coming toward me!

I quickly rolled up into a ball and tried to **hide** among the werewolf pumpkins.

I held my breath, hoping that the Cat Phantom would think I was just another pumpkin. I watched as the cat SHADOW came closer and closer. He stopped and LOOKED around. But he didn't find me!

Great Gouda, was I happy to be wearing Creepella's pumpkin costume!

Then I realized something. The Cat Phantom was holding a big pair of pruning shears in his paws — those big scissors used by gardeners. I could see them sparkling in the moonlight.

Creepella was right! That Cat Phantom was going to cut the stalks of the werewolf pumpkins and steal them!

What could I do?

Just then the werewolf pumpkins began to stir. They jumped on the cat, gnashing their teeth. Nom, nom, nom!

They attacked the Cat Phantom and bit his tail! He let out a loud . . .

I gasped.

CATS DON'T SAY "SQUEAK"! AND GHOSTS DON'T YELL "OUCH"!

Was this Cat Phantom really a cat? Was it really a phantom? Whatever he was, he ran out of the garden as the werewolf pumpkins hopped along after him.

You're safe.

1.

I slowly approached the pumpkins. Luckily, none of them had been hurt.

1. I gently **patted** them. "It's all right. You're safe now," I said. They moved their **leaves** to answer me with the pumpkin alphabet. "**Thanks, Geronimo.**"

2. Then I spotted something on the ground. That something was a **furry** fake cat tail! It had a **BITE** from one of the werewolf pumpkins!

2.

What's this?

It's a clue!

3. Holey cheese, it was a **CLUE**! This was **proof** that the thief was neither a **cat** nor a **phantom**! I **ran** toward the castle, holding the fake tail. I had to **alert** the Cacklefur family at once!

Pant...
Pant...

A Trap for the Cat Phantom!

When I reached the castle, Boneham was banging the gong to call everyone to midnight dinner.

GOOOOOOOOONG!

"Creepella!" I yelled.

She ran up to me. "Gerrykins, what is it? Tell me everything," she said. She pulled me aside so we could talk without being **overheard**. I told her what had happened and showed her the *fake* cat tail

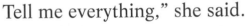

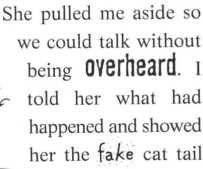

with the **bite** taken out of it.

"This **proves** that the **Cat Phantom** isn't real," I said. "It is probably one of the _____!"

"You're right," Creepella agreed. "But **which one**? You won't believe this, but all three guests showed up to dinner with **BANDAGED** tails. Which one of them was bitten by a **werewolf pumpkins**?"

"Let's interrogate them!" I suggested.

I approached **GASPAR**.

Strange!

Huh?

"How did you HURT your tail?" I asked him.

He sighed. "I crushed it in one of the **coffins** in Boris's collection."

Hmmm. Was that true?

Then I asked Alvin, "How did you HURT yourself?"

"I was taking a sample of **SLIME** from the piranha pond when one of them jumped up and bit me!" he answered.

Hmmm. Was that true?

Finally, I turned to Felix Bloomfur. "What

happened to you?" I asked.

"Well, I was walking through the **greenhouse** when I was attacked by some ~~carnivorous~~ ~~raspberries~~," he replied.

Ouch! That hurts!

Hmmm. Was that true?

"One of them has to be **LYING**," I said.

Creepella nodded. "You're right," she said. "But I have a thought: Whoever is the **Cat Phantom** had to quickly take off his **COSTUME** to get to the dining room in time. Maybe the thief left the **PROOF** in his room!"

"Brilliant!" I said. "Let's go check the rooms."

We walked up the Tower of the Headless Ghost and entered Alvin Testerly's room. The floor was tracked with **muddy** foot prints!

"Does this prove that Alvin was in the **pumpkin garden**?" I asked.

Creepella shook her head. "Alvin is always in the mud looking for **mutant viruses**," she said. "That doesn't mean it was him."

We investigated Gaspar Ghostine's room

next and saw that he had a **white cloak** hanging from the coat rack — just like the one worn by the **Cat Phantom**!

"Maybe it was Gaspar I saw in the **pumpkin garden**!" I exclaimed.

Creepella sighed. "That doesn't *prove* anything for sure. Gaspar is filming a movie here about a *ghost*. This could be one of his costumes."

Finally, we **CHECKED OUT** Felix Bloomfur's room. Right away, we spotted a pair of pruning shears on the floor!

"Look!" I cried. "The Cat Phantom had a pair just like this!"

Creepella shook her head. "But Felix is a GARDENER. He always uses pruning shears. It doesn't mean he's guilty!"

"Moldy mozzarella, this is frustrating!" I exclaimed.

Who could
it be?

"You're right," Creepella agreed. "There must be a way to tell the **REAL THIEF** from the other guests."

Then an **IDEA** hit me like a bolt of **lightning**. "Creepella, I think I know a way, but I need your **HELP**," I said. "Write a note to each of your admirers, and ask them to take a **MOONLIGHT** walk with you in the garden of the werewolf pumpkins."

She looked confused. "How will this help us **figure out** who the thief is, Gerrykins?"

"You'll see," I promised. **"TRUST ME!"**

So Creepella wrote **THREE NOTES**, and slipped one under the door of each guest's room.

My dear guest,
I am inviting you to take a moonlight walk with me at half-past midnight in the werewolf pumpkin garden . . . just you, me, and the pumpkins! Please don't keep me waiting!

Gloomily yours,

CREEPELLA

Then we **ran** to the garden, and Creepella warned the pumpkins, "Don't move until I say so!"

"Why don't you wait here, by the **pumpkin tent**," I suggested, "and I will hide here among the pumpkins. If my plan works, we will find out who the guilty one is!"

We waited. First, Alvin Testerly appeared on the path. He stepped toward Creepella.

"Oh, Creepella! What a romantic note you sent," he whispered.

Then . . . **OOf**! He
TRIPPED on one of the
cords of the **pumpkin
tent** and landed right on
his snout.

BOOOIIING!

"He isn't the fake
phantom," I told Creepella.

Then Gaspar Ghostine came.
"Beautiful Creepella!" he
exclaimed. "My heart aches
for you like . . ."

OOf He tripped on
a cord and landed right
on his snout next to Alvin.

BOOOIIING!

"He isn't the **guilty** one,
either," I said. "It can only be one **rat**!"

Felix Bloomfur **ran** into the garden.

"I'm here, Creepella!" he cried, and he jumped right over the cord of the pumpkin tent — he knew it was there! **WHOOP!**

I jumped up out of my **hiding place** between the pumpkins and pointed to him. "There he is! **HE'S THE FAKE PHANTOM! IT'S FELIX BLOOMFUR!**"

"Werewolf pumpkins, get him!" Creepella commanded.

The pumpkins hopped after him and wrapped their vines around him. Then they showed him their sharp teeth.

NOM, NOM, NOM!

"**Galloping ghosts**, just admit you did it, Felix!" Creepella said.

"Yes, it was me! I admit it!" Felix yelled. "Now please tell the **werewolf pumpkins** not to bite my tail!"

"I will call them off, but you must **tell the truth**!" Creepella insisted.

A Rodent
in Disguise!

Then **FELIX BLOOMFUR** did something surprising. He took off his blond wig and his mirrored sunglasses. He put on a pair of dark sunglasses. I recognized him right away.

"I remember you! You are one of Madame No's bodyguards!" I cried.

"It's **true**," he confessed. "I work for *Madame No*, the Mega Director of EGO Corp. — the biggest company on Mouse Island."

FELIX BLOOMFUR

HIS TRUE IDENTITY!

"I am a plant expert," Felix continued. "I took the bodyguard job to pay for my plant experiments. When *Madame No* learned of my skills, she gave me this mission."

"What exactly does that GREEDY RODENT want?" I asked.

"She knows that *pumpkinus voracious chomperitus* only grows in the Cacklefur garden," Felix replied. "Madame No asked me to **steal** them so she could sell them to others for a **high price**. I got a cat phantom costume to scare you away and keep you off my trail."

Madame No!

Madame No is the Mega Director of the EGO: the Enormousely Giant Organization. This powerful company delves into many kinds of business, both honest and shady. Ask her a question, and she has only one answer: "*No!*"

Felix turned to me. "How did you **KNOW** it was me?"

1 "The night I slept in the garden, the **Cat Phantom** tripped on the cords of the tent," I explained.

2 "I knew that one of the three guests was guilty, but I didn't know who!

3 "I made sure each guest had to **PASS** the tent.

4 "You didn't trip because you **remembered** where the cords were, so I knew you had to be the guilty one!"

Creepella hugged me. "Gerrykins, **you did it**!"

Felix frowned. "What will happen to me?"

"You will go back to *Madame No*," Creepella said firmly, "and bring her this message: If you cross the Cacklefur family again, you will get your tail bitten!"

Then she clapped her paws and the **werewolf pumpkins** released Felix. He fell to his knees.

"Oh, Creepella, I know I *lied*, but my feelings for you are real," he said.

Oh, Creepella!

"That doesn't matter!" Creepella cried. "You are nothing but a liar and a *thief*, and you work for a rodent with a heart more rotten than the **moldiest cheese**. You do not deserve to be on my **LIST** of admirers!"

She took her diary from her pocket,

opened it, and put a big **X** across Felix Bloomfur's picture.

"**NOOOOOOO!**" he wailed, and then he burst into **tears**.

"Sorry, Felix," she said. "YOU SHOULD NEVER MESS WITH A CACKLEFUR!"

Then we walked back to the **castle**, leaving Felix behind. Overhead, the sky turned **pink** with the morning sunrise.

Creepella immediately jumped into her

Turbotomb. "Hop in, Gerrykins!" she said. "Now we can go back to **New Mouse City**. There's a *surprise* for you there."

"Surprise?" I asked.

She nodded. "That's why I brought you here. So you wouldn't find out."

"What kind of *surprise*?" I asked anxiously.

She smiled. "You'll find out **TONIGHT** at *The Rodent's Gazette*, at **midnight**, sharp!"

What surprise?

HAPPY NIGHT OF THE WEREWOLF PUMPKINS!

Creepella brought me to *The Rodent's Gazette* at **midnight** on the dot.

New Mouse City was **spooky** at night!

I opened the door to the office . . . and saw a room full of **MONSTERS**!

"Happy night of the werewolf pumpkins!" they yelled.

Heeeelp!!

HAPPY HALLOWEEN

"**HEEEEELP!**" I yelled, and then I fainted.

When I came to, Benjamin was fanning me with the hem of his *ghost costume*.

"It's okay, Uncle G," he said. "We *surprised* you! We put together a **HALLOWEEN PARTY** right here at *The Rodent's Gazette*! It was Creepella's idea. Do you like it?"

"Y-y-yes," I stammered. I couldn't believe all the **effort** everyone had put into the party!

There was **coffin-shaped** furniture, which must be what those strange rodents in **BLACK** had delivered. All kinds of Halloween-themed food covered a very long table. That must have been what **TRAP** was preparing in the kitchen that he didn't want me to see.

The result was truly mousetastic!

But the **best thing** was that my friends, family, and coworkers were there. Creepella's family came, and so did her admirers!

She introduced them to me, one by one. "Geronimo, you already know Alvin and Gaspar," she began. "But here is Baron von Slick, Byron Novello, Count Sylvania . . ."

My head began to spin. Holey cheese, how many admirers did she have?

Luckily, Thea and Mousita pulled me away. "Ger, there's a Halloween costume for you, too," Thea said. "A werewolf pumpkin costume!"

"Enough!" I protested. "I'M A MOUSE, NOT A PUMPKIN!"

"But, Geronimo, we made it especially for you," Mousita said.

"CREEPELLA suggested it," Thea said. "She

SPOOKY JOKES

What do you do with a green monster?

Ripen it!

Why don't skeletons go sky diving?

Because they don't have any guts!

What kind of mistakes do ghosts make?

Boo boos!

Who did the zombie invite to his party?

Anyone he could dig up!

said you make an adorable pumpkin."

I sighed and put on the costume. After all, it was **Halloween**!

Then I heard Creepella's voice. "Thrills and chills, let's get this party started!" she said. "It will be scary, scream-worthy, a real frightfest!"

Hooray!

"HOORAY FOR THE NIGHT OF THE WEREWOLF PUMPKINS!" everyone cheered. Then the bandleader announced, "Now it's time for the Candle Waltz! Who's ready to dance?"

Creepella approached me. "Gerrykins, this is my **favorite** waltz. Will you **dance** with me?"

I coughed. "Well, actually, I'm not much of a dancer."

She smiled. "I understand," she said. Then she raised her voice. "Who would like to **dance** with me?"

All her admirers raised their paws.

"Um, wait!" I said quickly. "I can give it a try. It's just one little waltz, right?"

CREEPELLA took my paw in hers, and we walked out onto the dance floor. "Let's get waltzing, Gerrykins!" she said.

I was a little nervous, but I just followed the music. Soon Creepella and I were spinning around the dance floor with the other party guests.

"It's so nice to dance with a good friend," Creepella said with a sigh.

I had to admit, I was having a really good time, even though the room was decorated with spooky stuff. The whole room was filled with laughter and music.

Maybe we will celebrate this day every year!

That is the word of Stilton, Geronimo Stilton.

Happy Halloween!

UNTIL THE NEXT ADVENTURE!

Be sure to read all my fabumouse adventures!

#1 Lost Treasure of the Emerald Eye

#2 The Curse of the Cheese Pyramid

#3 Cat and Mouse in a Haunted House

#4 I'm Too Fond of My Fur!

#5 Four Mice Deep in the Jungle

#6 Paws Off, Cheddarface!

#7 Red Pizzas for a Blue Count

#8 Attack of the Bandit Cats

#9 A Fabumouse Vacation for Geronimo

#10 All Because of a Cup of Coffee

#11 It's Halloween, You 'Fraidy Mouse!

#12 Merry Christmas, Geronimo!

#13 The Phantom of the Subway

#14 The Temple of the Ruby of Fire

#15 The Mona Mousa Code

#16 A Cheese-Colored Camper

#17 Watch Your Whiskers, Stilton!

#18 Shipwreck on the Pirate Islands

#19 My Name Is Stilton, Geronimo Stilton

#20 Surf's Up, Geronimo!

#21 The Wild, Wild West

#22 The Secret of Cacklefur Castle

A Christmas Tale

#23 Valentine's Day Disaster

#24 Field Trip to Niagara Falls

#25 The Search for Sunken Treasure

#26 The Mummy with No Name

#27 The Christmas Toy Factory

#28 Wedding Crasher

#29 Down and Out Down Under

#30 The Mouse Island Marathon

#31 The Mysterious Cheese Thief

Christmas Catastrophe

#32 Valley of the Giant Skeletons

#33 Geronimo and the Gold Medal Mystery

#34 Geronimo Stilton, Secret Agent

#35 A Very Merry Christmas

#36 Geronimo's Valentine

#37 The Race Across America

#38 A Fabumouse School Adventure

#39 Singing Sensation

#40 The Karate Mouse

#41 Mighty Mount Kilimanjaro

#42 The Peculiar Pumpkin Thief

#43 I'm Not a Supermouse!

#44 The Giant Diamond Robbery

#45 Save the White Whale!

#46 The Haunted Castle

#47 Run for the Hills, Geronimo!

#48 The Mystery in Venice

#49 The Way of the Samurai

#50 This Hotel Is Haunted!

#51 The Enormouse Pearl Heist

#52 Mouse in Space!

#53 Rumble in the Jungle

#54 Get into Gear, Stilton!

#55 The Golden Statue Plot

#56 Flight of the Red Bandit

#57 The Stinky Cheese Vacation

#58 The Super Chef Contest

#59 Welcome to Moldy Manor

#60 The Treasure of Easter Island

#61 Mouse House Hunter

#62 Mouse Overboard!

#63 The Cheese Experiment

#64 Magical Mission

#65 Bollywood Burglary

#66 Operation: Secret Recipe

#67 The Chocolate Chase

#68 Cyber-Thief Showdown

#69 Hug a Tree, Geronimo

#70 The Phantom Bandit

Don't miss any of my adventures in the Kingdom of Fantasy!

THE KINGDOM OF FANTASY

THE QUEST FOR PARADISE:
THE RETURN TO THE KINGDOM OF FANTASY

THE AMAZING VOYAGE:
THE THIRD ADVENTURE IN THE KINGDOM OF FANTASY

THE DRAGON PROPHECY:
THE FOURTH ADVENTURE IN THE KINGDOM OF FANTASY

THE VOLCANO OF FIRE:
THE FIFTH ADVENTURE IN THE KINGDOM OF FANTASY

THE SEARCH FOR TREASURE:
THE SIXTH ADVENTURE IN THE KINGDOM OF FANTASY

THE ENCHANTED CHARMS:
THE SEVENTH ADVENTURE IN THE KINGDOM OF FANTASY

THE PHOENIX OF DESTINY:
AN EPIC KINGDOM OF FANTASY ADVENTURE

THE HOUR OF MAGIC:
THE EIGHTH ADVENTURE IN THE KINGDOM OF FANTASY

THE WIZARD'S WAND:
THE NINTH ADVENTURE IN THE KINGDOM OF FANTASY

THE SHIP OF SECRETS:
THE TENTH ADVENTURE IN THE KINGDOM OF FANTASY

THE DRAGON OF FORTUNE:
AN EPIC KINGDOM OF FANTASY ADVENTURE

THE GUARDIAN OF THE REALM:
THE ELEVENTH ADVENTURE IN THE KINGDOM OF FANTASY

ABOUT THE AUTHOR

 Born in New Mouse City, Mouse Island, **GERONIMO STILTON** is Rattus Emeritus of Mousomorphic Literature and of Neo-Ratonic Comparative Philosophy. For the past twenty years, he has been running *The Rodent's Gazette*, New Mouse City's most widely read daily newspaper.

Stilton was awarded the Ratitzer Prize for his scoops on *The Curse of the Cheese Pyramid* and *The Search for Sunken Treasure*. He has also received the Andersen 2000 Prize for Personality of the Year. One of his bestsellers won the 2002 eBook Award for world's best ratlings' electronic book. His works have been published all over the globe.

In his spare time, Mr. Stilton collects antique cheese rinds and plays golf. But what he most enjoys is telling stories to his nephew Benjamin.

1. Main entrance
2. Printing presses (where the books and newspaper are printed)
3. Accounts department
4. Editorial room (where the editors, illustrators, and designers work)
5. Geronimo Stilton's office
6. Helicopter landing pad

THE RODENT'S
GAZETTE

Map of New Mouse City

Map of Mouse Island

Dear mouse friends,
Thanks for reading, and farewell
till the next book.
It'll be another whisker-licking-good
adventure, and that's a promise!

Geronimo Stilton